Book! Book! Book!

To my mother for her support
and my father for his humour
– D. B.

For Meike and Balder
With love
– T. B.

Scholastic Children's Books
Commonwealth House, 1-19 New Oxford Street,
London WC1A 1NU, UK
a division of Scholastic Ltd
London - New York - Toronto - Sydney - Auckland
Mexico City - New Delhi - Hong Kong

First published in hardback in the US by Scholastic Inc, New York, 2001
This paperback edition published by Scholastic Ltd, 2002

Text copyright © 2001 by Deborah Bruss
Illustrations copyright © 2001 by Tiphanie Beeke

ISBN 0 439 97935 8

Printed by Oriental Press, Dubai, UAE
All rights reserved

2 4 6 8 10 9 7 5 3 1

Book! Book! Book!

by Deborah Bruss

illustrated by Tiphanie Beeke

Down at the farm, all was well until . . .

. . . the children went back to school and the
animals had nothing to do.

They had no rides to share, no tug-of-war to play, no one to scratch behind their ears or ruffle their feathers.

In the bright morning sun, the horse hung his head,

the cow complained,

and the goat grumbled.

The pig pouted,

the duck dozed off,

and the hen heaved a sigh.

Around about noon, with the sun high above the barnyard, the hen squawked, "I'm bored! And I'm heading to town to find something to do!" The animals followed her down the road.

Library

"Look!" clucked the hen. "Happy faces. This must be the place we're looking for. I'll go in and see if I can find something to do."

"Neigh! Neigh!" whinnied the horse. "You're too small for such a big job. Leave it to me."

The horse clip-clopped in. Politely he asked for
something to do. But the librarian could not understand
the horse. All she heard was, "Neigh! Neigh!"
So the horse hung his head and clip-clopped out.

Next the cow plodded in. Politely she
asked for something to do. But the librarian
could not understand the cow.

All she heard was, **"Moo! Moo!"** So the
cow complained and plodded out.

Now it was the goat's turn, and *he* trotted in.
Politely he asked for something to do. But the
librarian could not understand the goat. All
she heard was, **"Baaah! Baaah!"** So the goat
grumbled and trotted out again.

Slowly the pig ambled into the library.
Politely she asked for something to do.

But all the librarian heard was,
"Oink! Oink!" So the pig ambled
out to tell her friends.

Up flapped the hen, and she announced,
"I am going in, and no one is going to stop
me!" Into the library she flapped.

"Book!" clucked the hen politely.

The librarian looked around and said,

"What's that noise?"

"Book! BOOK!" clucked the hen.

The librarian scratched her head. "Who's that?" she asked.

"Book! Book! BOOK!" clucked the hen quite clearly.

"Oh! Is this what you want?" asked the librarian,
and she handed the hen three books.

farm

Back at the farm, the horse, the cow, the goat, the pig, the duck and the hen gathered around the books.

The barnyard was filled with *neighs*, **moos**, **baaahs**, **oinks**, *quacks* and book-book-BOOKS! Their sounds of delight lasted until sundown.

All the animals were happy, except . . .

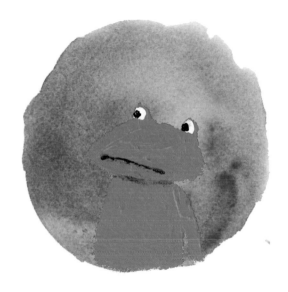

. . . for the bullfrog. And do you know what he said?

"I've already **read it!**
Read it, read it, read it . . ."